LITTLE WOLF'S
FIRST HOWLING

Laura McGee Kvasnosky
and Kate Harvey McGee

WALKER BOOKS
AND SUBSIDIARIES
LONDON · BOSTON · SYDNEY · AUCKLAND

LITTLE WOLF'S FATHER led the way straight to the top of the hill.

Little Wolf zigzagged behind, sniffing each stone and sage.

"Tonight's the night," said Big Wolf. "Your first howling."

Little Wolf's ears shivered with excitement. "I'm ready," he said.

"I am ready to howl!"

Father and son sat side by side. They watched as the stars
blinked on and a full moon peeked over the mountain.
"Is it time yet?" said Little Wolf. "Can I howl now?"
"Hold on," said his father, "First, let me demonstrate proper

Big Wolf stood tall. He took a deep breath.
He lifted his muzzle to the sky and howled.

AAAAAAAA

AAOOOOOOOOOOOOOOOOOOOOOOOOOOOOOOOOOOOO

The last notes drifted out over the valley.
Little Wolf was thrilled to the tip of his tail.
"My turn now. Right, Dad? Here I go. Just like you."
Big Wolf nodded. "OK, Son. Give it a try."

Little Wolf stood tall. He took a deep breath.
He lifted his muzzle to the sky and howled.

Big Wolf raised his eyebrows. "That was a good beginning," he said, "but your finish was not proper howling form. Let me demonstrate again."

AAAAAAAAAAAOOOOOO

"I got it. I got it," said Little Wolf.

Little Wolf lifted his muzzle to the sky and howled again.

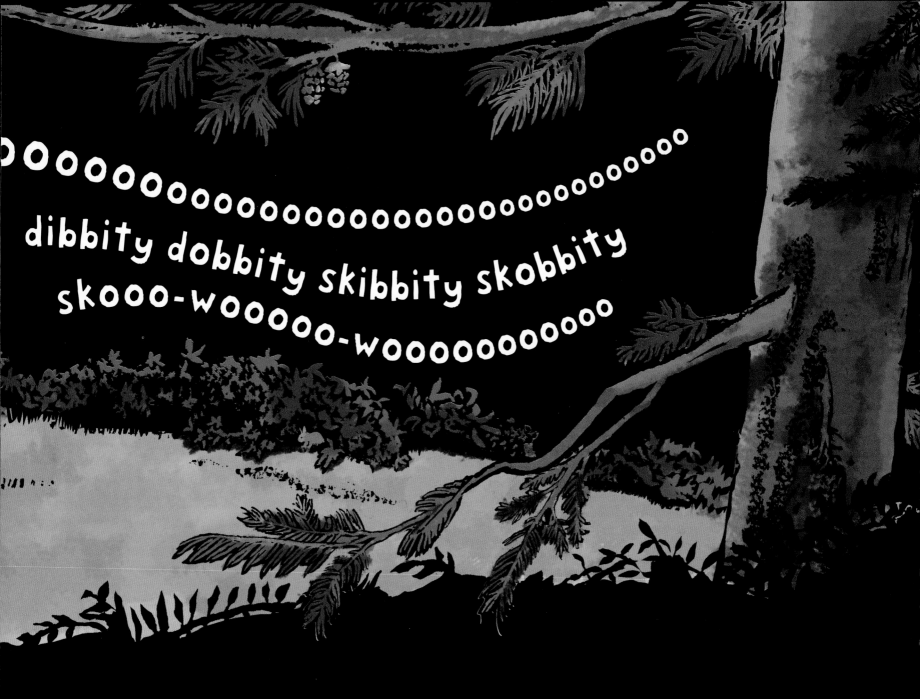

dibbity dobbity skibbity skobbity skooo-wooooo-wooooooooooo

Little Wolf looked over at his father. "What do you think, Dad?
Did you like it? Did you?"

Big Wolf sighed. "Son, I am proud of your nose which has led to many new trails. I admire your strength when you tumble with the other pups. Most of all, I love how your ears express your thoughts. But your howling? It is not proper howling form."

Little Wolf hung his head.

"Let me demonstrate again," said Big Wolf.
"Listen closely."

AAAA

AAAAAOOOOOOOOOOOOOOOOOOOO

Each note rang clear and true and soared to the moon.

Little Wolf's heart swelled with wildness and joy. He knew
it wasn't proper howling form, but he had to let loose.

skiddily skoddily beep bop, a bo
boppita boppita wheeee bop,

oo booo boooooooooooooooooooooooooooooooo

diddily daddily dooooooooooooooooooooooooooo

Big Wolf listened closely.
His tail started wagging.
His ears started twitching.
His paws started tapping.
Big Wolf couldn't help it.

DIBBY, DIBBY DO-WOP A DOOOOOOOO!

Little Wolf grinned from ear to furry ear and howled back.

dibby, dibby do-wop a dooooooooo!

OOOO

DILY DADDILY DOOO

skobbity skooooo-wooo-wooooo

OOWLING, 'OWLING TO THE MOOOOON!

Together they howled the moon to the top of the sky.

Little Wolf stuck close to his father as they trotted home.
"Wait until we tell the others," said Little Wolf.
Big Wolf smiled. "Oh, I expect they already know."